The Fairy House

Fairy Flying Lessons

Welcome to the Fairy House –
a whole new magical world...

Have you got all *The Fairy House* books?

☐ FAIRY FRIENDS
☐ FAIRY FOR A DAY
☐ FAIRIES TO THE RESCUE
☐ FAIRY RIDING SCHOOL
☐ FAIRY SLEEPOVER
☐ FAIRY JEWELS
☐ FAIRY PARTY
☐ FAIRY FLYING LESSONS

Make sure you visit www.thefairyhouse.co.uk
for competitions, prizes and lots more fairy fun!

The Fairy House

Fairy Flying Lessons

Kelly McKain

Illustrated by Nicola Slater

SCHOLASTIC

First published in the UK in 2008 by Scholastic Children's Books
An imprint of Scholastic Ltd
Euston House, 24 Eversholt Street
London, NW1 1DB, UK
Registered office: Westfield Road, Southam, Warwickshire, CV47 0RA
SCHOLASTIC and associated logos are trademarks and or registered trademarks of Scholastic Inc.
This edition published in 2009

ISBN 978 1 407 10893 3

A C   ʼbrary

This is a work of fiction. Names, characters, places, incidents and dialogues are products
of the author's imagination or are used fictitiously. Any resemblance to actual
people, living or dead, events or locales is entirely coincidental.

www.kellymckain.co.uk
www.scholastic.co.uk/zone

For

Tabitha Sophie,
and her proud parents

Chapter 1

The summer rain splashed down, bouncing off the patio table in Katie's back garden.

"Are you sure you want to play outside in this weather, darling?" asked Mum, as Katie pulled on her wellies.

"Oh, yes, I don't mind getting wet," said Katie, grinning to herself as she did up the buttons of her bright-yellow raincoat.

Mum sighed and gave her a

goodbye hug. "Well, don't be too long, darling," she said. "Let's have an early lunch and then perhaps we can watch a film together."

"OK, that sounds great," said Katie. Mum worried that she hadn't made any friends in their new village yet, and she tried to make up for it by filling the long summer holidays with fun things to do like watching films, painting, cooking and visits to Auntie Jane.

As Katie dashed across the back garden in her raincoat and wellies, she wished she could tell Mum that she *had* made some new friends. *Four* new friends, in fact.

Well, she *had* tried to tell Mum about them but, being a grown-up, Mum had assumed that they were only in her imagination. Katie ducked under the wire fence into the

almost-meadow and breathed in the sweet smell of the rain on the lush green grass. Underneath the old oak tree stood Katie's dolls' house.

This was where her four friends lived.

And they were *fairies*.

Katie crouched down beside the little house, which looked so cosy with the cheerful polka dot curtains

hanging in the windows and the soft glow of the daisy lights beyond. She touched the tiny blue door handle with the very tip of her little finger and whispered the magic words, "I believe in fairies, I believe in fairies, I believe in fairies." She squealed with excitement as the top of her head tingled. Then a great whooshing sound roared in her ears and she shrank down and down and down . . . to fairy size!

Katie hurried into the Fairy House and her friends rushed up to greet her. Daisy, the kind summer fairy, fussed around her, pulling off her wet coat and finding her a scrap of material to dry her hair on.

Boisterous Bluebell, the spring fairy and the naughtiest of the four by far, tried to pull off her wellies. But they were very stuck, so then

Rosehip, the fiery autumn fairy with the flame-red hair, gave Bluebell a hand. Snowdrop, the shy winter fairy, grinned out from beneath her sweep of sleek black hair and said, "We've been making something, come and see."

Intrigued, Katie followed them into the kitchen, shuffling along in her socks. Then she gasped in amazement. There, laid out on the table, were the most beautiful trinkets she'd ever seen. The fairies had been working very, very hard indeed.

"They're lucky charm bracelets," said Snowdrop.

The bracelets were made of wild flowers and grass stems woven together, with crystal beads and silver stars from Katie's craft set threaded on to them. Katie picked one up and was surprised to find that the flowers were solid to the touch, as though made of wire and silk.

"We put a sprinkle of fairy dust on to them," Rosehip explained, "so that the flowers will last for ever."

"No one will ever realize that the little bit of extra sparkle is *real* fairy dust!" giggled Rosehip.

"They're beautiful," Katie gasped. "Can I have a go at making one?"

They all sat down around the table and Daisy showed Katie how to thread the beads on to the wild flowers.

"You know, we're making them *for* something," said Bluebell, looking very pleased with herself. "You see, we've had an idea."

She looked at Snowdrop who explained, "If you put these bracelets on when you turn big again, they'll turn big too, and then you could show them to your mum and persuade her to let you sell

them at her art exhibition on Saturday."

"Do you think we'd be able to make enough money to buy another one of the birthstones?" asked Daisy, as she threaded beads on to a grass stem.

"Some of them are very expensive," Katie said, "like diamond and emerald, but we might be able to afford a piece of turquoise or amethyst."

"Brilliant!" cried Snowdrop.

"So then we'll be even closer to completing the fairy task," finished Rosehip triumphantly.

Katie nodded. She knew how important the fairy task was to her friends. She glanced up at the Fairy Queen's message which Snowdrop had stuck on to the kitchen cupboard.

Fairy Task No. 45826

By Royal Command of the Fairy Queen

Terrible news has reached Fairyland. As you
know, the Magic Oak is the gateway between
Fairyland and the human world. The
sparkling whirlwind can only drop fairies off
here. Humans plan to knock down our special
tree and build a house on the land. If this
happens, fairies will no longer be able to
come and help people and the environment.
You must stop them from doing this terrible
thing and make sure that the tree is
protected for the future. Only then will you
be allowed back into Fairyland.

By order of Her Eternal Majesty
The Fairy Queen

PS You will need one each of the twelve
birthstones to work the magic that will
save the tree - but hurry, there's not
much time!

9

Katie and the fairies had already collected seven of the birthstones, and they needed five more. They had also discovered who was behind the plans to knock down the tree and build a luxury villa in the almost-meadow. It was Max Towner, Tiffany Towner's father. Tiffany was a horrible bully in Katie's class who had stopped the other girls from playing with her.

Katie and the fairies didn't know exactly when Max Towner was planning to knock the tree down, but they were desperately trying to collect all the birthstones as quickly as they could.

Katie couldn't even bear to think about what would happen if they didn't work the magic in time. But she was sure of one thing – if earth and Fairyland were cut off from one

another it would be a disaster. After all, if the fairies could no longer come down the sparkling whirlwind, who would look after all the trees and flowers and animals?

Suddenly there was a BANG and a CRASH outside, which made them all jump.

For a moment Katie thought that Max Towner had come crashing in with the digger already.

Rosehip flew over to the window and

looked out. "It's a bird," she gasped, "and, oh dear, he's hurt his wing."

Daisy and Snowdrop went over to look as well. Then, "Aaaaaahhhhhh!" they screamed and shot back across the room and under the table.

"What's wrong?" Bluebell demanded. "Whatever it is, it can't be *that* scary! Let *me* have a look." And with that, she zoomed over to the window and peered out.

"AAAAAAAAHHHHHHHH!!!" she screamed. She dived under the table too. "A cat!" she whispered. "It's enormous!"

Bang! Flap, flap, bang!

They all clung together in terror as the bird threw himself against the side of the Fairy House, making the whole thing shudder and shake.

"We have to help him!" cried Rosehip. "If we don't, that cat is

going to get hold of him and. . ." She trailed off with a shudder. She crept out from under the table and began a wobbly flutter across the kitchen to the hallway . . . and the front door.

"Rosehip, you can't!" cried Daisy.

"It's OK," called Rosehip. "If I'm quick I can open the door and—"

But just then the cat took another swipe at the bird and its big ginger paw battered the side of the Fairy House. They all screamed. The house tipped up and rocked back and forth, almost falling on to its side. Rosehip pleaded with her friends, almost in tears. "I can't open the door if the

house falls over. We have to do something! We have to help the bird!"

"We can't!" cried Snowdrop.

"It's too dangerous," Daisy agreed.

But Bluebell looked determined. "OK, I'll distract the cat," she said. "Just wait for my signal, then open the door."

Rosehip nodded and flew off.

Bluebell took a deep breath, then flew upstairs and out of her bedroom window. Terrified for her, Katie, Daisy and Snowdrop crept to the kitchen window and peered out. They gasped as Bluebell zoomed round near the cat, just out of its reach. They shrieked as its claws came slashing through the air right beside her. All the cat's attention was on her. "Now!" she called, and Rosehip opened the front door.

The flame-haired fairy shrieked and threw herself to the floor as the bird came crashing in. He skittered across the hallway, flapping his wings in panic, and squeezed through the doorway into the kitchen. Rosehip dived back under the table and huddled together with the others, trembling. The banging and crashing and flapping and skittering was right above their heads. Poor little Snowdrop looked absolutely terrified and Daisy held her tight. Just then, Bluebell zoomed back down the stairs and appeared at the kitchen door.

"Quick," she cried. "Let's hide!"

They grabbed each other's hands and hurried out, shielding their faces as the bird flapped beside them. Just then the cat threw itself at the Fairy House to try and reach the bird. Its

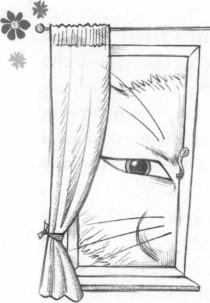

angry yowl pierced the air. Katie stared in fright at the enormous eye looking in the window. As the cat moved she saw the tag on its collar.

As Katie tugged Daisy upstairs, she hissed, "That's Tiffany's cat! Typical! He's as mean as she is!"

"PUSSKINS"
I belong to
Tiffany Towner
834 9926

"What if Tiffany's nearby?" said Rosehip. "She could be even more dangerous than her cat!"

"I didn't see her when I went out," said Bluebell. "I think the cat has just ended up here after chasing the bird."

"I really hope you're right," said Daisy with a shudder.

They squeezed into their favourite hiding place, Snowdrop's wardrobe, and huddled together in the dark, listening to the bangs and crashes of the bird skittering downstairs. They screamed every time the cat's paw batted the Fairy House – almost tipping it over as the cat tried to get to the bird.

Now the bird was panicking and flapping around the living room. Rosehip winced as he leapt on to the piano with a *twang*! "I hope he hasn't broken it," she murmured.

They held each other tight again, squealing, as the cat pounced once more and the whole house teetered on the brink of falling.

"What if that cat manages to push the house over and we all fall out and get eaten up?" cried Daisy. They'd all been thinking that, but hearing it said out loud made Snowdrop burst into tears.

They stayed in the wardrobe, huddled together, until finally the house stopped shaking and there was silence from downstairs.

"Maybe the cat gave up and went away," whispered Rosehip.

Bluebell put a finger to her lips, then opened the wardrobe door and crept out. She went to the window and peered nervously out into the almost-meadow. "Yes it's OK, the cat's gone," she told them.

She flew around, looking out of every upstairs window to make absolutely sure, and then finally the other fairies felt brave enough to come out of the wardrobe.

Holding each others' hands tightly, they crept downstairs, very nervous about what they might find.

Chapter 2

First of all, Katie and the fairies tiptoed into the kitchen. The bird was not there, but. . .

"Oh no!" wailed Snowdrop. "The lucky charms!"

Flowers and stars and crystal beads were strewn all over the floor and not a single lucky charm bracelet was left in one piece.

"The bird must have broken them by accident, flapping around like that," said Rosehip.

Snowdrop bent to pick up a scrap of beaded daisy chain, then let it fall through her fingers. "There won't be time to make them all over again before Saturday," she murmured. She blinked back tears and Daisy put her arm around her. "Our plan's ruined!" she cried. "How are we going to get another birthstone now?"

Rosehip looked upset too, but she said, "We'll just have to forget about that for the moment. Shh! Listen. The bird needs our help."

They all heard quiet crying, and followed it into the living room. They gasped when they saw the mess. The little table had been turned over and the daisy lamp was broken. The rose-petal rug was ripped in half and the pressed flower pictures had fallen off the walls and lay in a heap on the floor.

And there, hiding behind the sofa, crying softly, was the bird.

Bluebell hurried over to comfort him but he just screeched and flapped his wings, then hid again. She squealed and dashed back to the others in the doorway.

"Bluebell! Can't you see he's frightened!" hissed Rosehip. "You can't just go charging up to him!"

"But *we're* not the ones who've frightened him!" Bluebell protested.

"It was that horrible cat! Besides, he's bigger than all of us – we should be frightened of *him*!"

"We are!" said Daisy with a shudder.

"Yes, we are!" echoed Snowdrop. "He's very strong. Look what he did to our lovely living room!"

"He didn't mean to," said Rosehip gently. "He's more frightened of you than you are of him."

"I doubt that," said Daisy darkly.

But Rosehip took a step into the room.

"Don't go up to him," Snowdrop warned.

"I'm not going to," she assured them. "I'm going to let him come to me. Stay here." And with that she crept into the room, and tiptoed to the farthest corner, away from the bird. Then she sat down quietly.

And she sat. And she sat some more.

The others hovered nervously in the doorway.

After a few minutes, Bluebell sighed impatiently. "Rosehip, it's not working!" she hissed.

"You shouldn't be in there, it's dangerous," added Daisy.

"And we don't have time to stand here doing nothing," said Snowdrop. "We need to work out how to get another birthstone. We've got a very important fairy task to do, remember?"

But Rosehip just smiled at them and put her finger to her lips. "Listen," she breathed. They all listened and Katie realized that the bird had stopped crying.

A few moments later, he stuck his head out from behind the sofa again, sending Snowdrop leaping into Daisy's arms. But Rosehip stayed where she was. She began to sing quietly to herself, under her breath.

After a few minutes the bird took a couple of hops into the centre of the room.

"He's a magpie," whispered Katie. "Look, he's still quite fluffy, that means he's only young. His adult feathers haven't all come in yet."

It only took him another couple of hops to get over to Rosehip.

"Rosehip, get up, he's going to squash you!" hissed Daisy.

"Yes, hurry, Rosehip!" echoed Bluebell. Even the bravest little fairy was worried about her friend now.

But Rosehip just smiled and

continued to sing, a little more loudly. The bird cocked his head to one side and listened. After another few minutes he stretched up and flapped his wings. Rosehip stayed where she was. They all held their breath. Then he sat down, not *on* her, but beside her. They all breathed out. Soon Rosehip was stroking the bird's soft black and white feathers and singing to him.

Katie couldn't believe her eyes.

She had seen Rosehip talk to a pony before, but she'd never have imagined that her friend could speak to a wild bird!

And the bird was answering her with a soft call that went *chacker-chacker-chacker*. It reminded Katie of the sound of maracas being shaken.

After a while Rosehip motioned to the others to come in. "It's OK, don't be scared, he's much calmer now," she told them.

They crept closer and sat down quietly a little distance away, on the remains of the rose-petal rug. Soon Rosehip had the bird's head in her lap and she was stroking his feathers and picking out the silver stars and bits of lucky charm that were still stuck to them. As she soothed and calmed him she told the others what he had said. "He

only just learned to fly a few weeks ago and he was sticking close to his mummy and daddy by the nest," she told them. "And then one day when he was on the ground the cat crept up and pounced on him. That's how his wing got hurt. He tried to fly away as fast as he could but because of his injured wing the cat almost caught him. Luckily he ended up here."

Rosehip gently lifted the bird's wing and examined it. "It's not broken, but it is very sore," she said, first to the bird and then to her friends.

"*Chacker-chacker-chacker,*" called the bird.

"And he bumped his head!" Rosehip added.

"Aw! Poor thing!" said Daisy, forgetting to be frightened.

"Does he have a name?" asked Katie.

Rosehip asked the bird and then shook her head. "He doesn't know," she told them.

Katie frowned. "Everyone should have a name," she said. "Let's give him one. How about Lucky, because he had a lucky escape!"

"Yes, *and* because he's covered in bits of lucky charm!" added Bluebell.

They all agreed to call the magpie Lucky, and when Rosehip told him this, he puffed up his feathers with pride.

"Wait a minute," said Snowdrop. She slipped out of the room and flew upstairs. In a few moments she came back with one of the polka dot curtains from her bedroom. "I thought we could make him a

sling," she explained, "for his poorly wing."

"What a lovely idea, Snowdrop," said Rosehip, and the pale winter fairy blushed with pride.

The fairies and Katie shuffled closer to the bird. Snowdrop helped Rosehip to put his wing into a home-made sling, and Katie stroked his back while Daisy and Bluebell carefully bandaged his head.

They all jumped as Lucky let out a long, pitiful cry.

"He wants to get back to his mummy and daddy," said Rosehip. "They must think the cat got him. He needs to let them know he's OK."

Their fear forgotten, Katie and the fairies fussed and stroked the fluffy bird. "Rosehip, say we'll help him get back to his parents," said Katie.

Rosehip frowned. "But we can't promise him that. We don't even know where the nest is. And what if his wing doesn't get better?"

But Katie looked so desperate that Rosehip promised Lucky they'd get him home. That calmed him down a little, and after lots more cuddling and stroking and soft fairy singing he fell into an exhausted sleep.

Rosehip put her finger to her lips and ushered them all out into the kitchen. "Katie, I don't know how we can—" she began, in a whisper, but Katie interrupted her.

"We *have* to get him home, Rosehip. His parents will be desperately worried about him. I just keep thinking . . . If I couldn't get back to Mum . . . Well, I can imagine how awful it would feel. Somehow, we have to get him home. We just *have* to."

Chapter 3

As soon as Katie got back to the house for lunch, she told Mum what had happened. "We were all inside the Fairy House and a young bird crashed in through the door," she said breathlessly, "well, because Rosehip was brave and held it open, because Tiffany's cat was after him, and we were all hiding in the wardrobe and the cat was prowling round outside and then at last it went away and we

had to go down and help the bird and—"

Katie stopped short. Mum was grinning at her as she placed a steaming hot bowl of pasta on the table. "That sounds like a lovely game, darling," she said. "What a brilliant imagination you've got. Now, come on, wash your hands."

"But, I—" Katie began, then she sighed and shuffled off to the bathroom. Like most grown-ups, Mum didn't believe in fairies. That

meant she couldn't see Rosehip, Bluebell, Daisy and Snowdrop, even when they were fluttering right in front of her eyes. So there was no point trying to convince her that Lucky was real. But still, Katie knew she could always bring him in to Mum and ask for her help if they needed it.

After they had eaten all the tuna pasta bake, they took their bowls of home-grown strawberries into the living room and watched a film together. It eventually stopped raining and when the film was over Katie asked if she could go back out to the almost-meadow. She was keen to check on Lucky.

"Of course you can, darling," said Mum. "I hope you don't get too lonely playing by yourself, though."

"Oh, no, I won't," said Katie, with a twinkle in her eye.

When Katie arrived back at the Fairy House, she turned small and hurried through the front door. The fairies had put things straight in the house as best they could. But they all looked very worried. And Lucky was wailing at the top of his voice.

"He's saying he's hungry," said Bluebell with a frown.

"I did make him some fairy cakes," said Daisy, pointing to a plate of beautiful cakes with jewel-coloured icing, which were hovering just above the plate, as fairy cakes do.

"But he wouldn't touch them," Snowdrop explained.

"Even *I* don't know what to do," Rosehip admitted.

"He won't want *cakes*," Katie told

them. "That's not what birds eat."

Bluebell folded her arms crossly. "Well, we didn't know!" she said sniffily. "What *do* they eat then?"

"Worms," said Katie, and the fairies all squirmed and squealed in disgust.

YUCK!

"Worms?" Snowdrop shrieked. "But that's *revolting*!"

Katie shrugged. "Not if you're a bird! Rosehip, go and calm him down, say we're going to find him some food and we'll be back very soon."

Snowdrop looked at her in horror.

"But we're not actually going to. . ." she began.

"That's right, we're going to look for worms," Katie said. "Except Rosehip, she ought to stay here and look after Lucky."

Rosehip smiled a smug smile and Bluebell stamped her foot crossly. "But that's not fair, how come she doesn't have to come and pick up smelly, slimy, wriggly worms?"

Katie frowned at them. "Oh, come on, girls! It's not my idea of fun either but you do want to help Lucky, don't you?"

Eventually they all mumbled that they did.

And with that they set off across the almost-meadow, with Rosehip waving them goodbye from the doorstep.

"The rain's just stopped, so it's

the perfect time to find worms,"
Katie told them.

"Oh *good*," muttered Daisy, not
meaning it at all.

They swished through the tall,
wet grass, which came up past their
heads, poking nervously around in
the soil until. . .

"Argh! Over here!" screamed
Snowdrop.

She had found a really fat juicy
worm. It wriggled and wriggled and
the fairies squealed as they picked it up.
They staggered a few steps with it,

shrieking and complaining. And then, "Argh!" squealed Bluebell, "it's going down my neck!"

They couldn't help giggling then. Even Bluebell saw the funny side and joined in. Carrying the worm wasn't so bad after that. They struggled back to the Fairy House and brought it into the living room to show Rosehip.

"Should we bake it in a pie or something?" Daisy asked, but before anyone could answer, Lucky had grabbed it and gulped it down.

"Yuck! I'm glad we eat cakes!" cried Snowdrop with a shudder.

Lucky was much happier after gobbling up the worm, though. And when he snuggled up to Snowdrop to say thank you for finding it, she couldn't help smiling.

"Poor thing, he's very dirty and

scruffy after that mean cat chased him," said Rosehip.

"Hmm. Let me just check something," said Katie. She hurried to the window and peered out. "Yes, I thought so. The bath tub is still outside from when we were making wild strawberry juice in it and it's filled up with rainwater."

"It would make a perfect bird bath!" cried Rosehip. "Good thinking, Katie!"

Rosehip gently coaxed Lucky outside and into the bath tub. Daisy made a shower cap out of a jam jar cover to protect his bandage, and Snowdrop sprinkled some fairy dust into the water so that it glistened with sparkly silver bubbles. A few moments later Lucky was happily splashing around while the fairies washed him with wild

strawberry shampoo. Even Snowdrop
and Daisy weren't scared of him any
more, and they gently cleaned the
glue off his feathers where the silver
stars had got stuck.

Katie and Bluebell sponged the
mud from his legs and Rosehip
poured rinsing water over his back
with an acorn cup. When he was all
nice and clean, they made a big fuss
of him for being well behaved.

Lucky hopped out of the tub and flapped his good wing. This sprayed water all over the fairies, soaking them, and they fell about giggling.

Soon they were all indoors, towelling Lucky dry and getting him warm. Then Daisy went upstairs, brought down the big yellow quilt she had embroidered with a happy smiling Mr Sunshine and gave it to him to snuggle up in.

When he was cosy and calm, Katie and the fairies crept out of the room and into the kitchen. "Well done, Rosehip, you were brilliant," said Daisy, and they all had a big fairy hug.

"Well done all of us," said Rosehip firmly. "We saved Lucky's life and that's something to be really proud of. Now we just have

to hope his wing gets better, so that he can fly back to his mummy and daddy."

Chapter 4

The next morning, the sun was shining and Katie hurried out to the Fairy House as soon as she'd had breakfast. When she turned small and went inside, she was surprised to find that the fairies had only just changed out of their pyjamas. Instead of greeting her with their usual chatter and hugs, they were all yawning and rubbing their eyes.

"We hardly got any sleep last night!" grumbled Bluebell. "We did

try to go to bed, but Lucky got upset without us and in the end we had to bring our quilts downstairs and all sleep together."

Katie secretly thought this sounded great fun, almost like a sleepover, and she was upset that she'd missed it. That was until Daisy said, "He kept trying to cuddle up with us, but because he's so big, we got really squashed!" That didn't sound so good after all.

Even Rosehip stifled a yawn and muttered, "We'll have to get him back to his mummy and daddy if we ever want any sleep! Come on, let's undo the sling and see how his wing feels. Maybe he'll be able to fly now."

They shuffled through to the living room and there was Lucky,

still cuddled up in the pile of quilts, snoring loudly.

They woke him up and Rosehip spoke softly to him. They undid the sling and unwound the bandage. He stood up and did a few hops, then he called something to Rosehip. "He says he feels fine now," she told them. "He wants to try flying back to the nest."

So Bluebell double-checked that the cat wasn't lurking about, and then Rosehip and Katie led Lucky outside. He smelt the air and looked warily around, then chacker-chackered something to Rosehip.

"He says he doesn't know where the nest is," said Rosehip anxiously. "He must have come really far when he was being chased by the cat."

"Tell him not to worry," said

Katie gently, stroking Lucky's head. "When he gets up into the air I'm sure he'll spot it."

"*Chacker-chacker-chacker*," Lucky called. Rosehip turned to translate but Katie could already tell that he wanted his mum.

"Come on, then, try your wings," Katie said, flapping her own arms encouragingly and doing a few hops. Rosehip sang this to Lucky and he flapped his wings cautiously, hopping up and down. But nothing much happened, and he didn't even leave the ground.

"It's OK, just have another go," said Katie, not feeling too worried. She knew it would take Lucky a while to get the hang of flying again.

Lucky flapped his wings and hopped from one leg to the other . . . but still nothing happened.

He tried again. Again nothing happened. And again. And again.

After half an hour, he still couldn't get into the air.

By now Katie and the fairies were feeling very worried indeed.

"I don't know what to do," Rosehip cried, on the verge of tears. "He still can't fly, even though his wing's better. I think he's lost his confidence after being chased by that horrible cat."

The five friends made a fairy huddle and had a quick talk about what to do.

"We need to come up with an idea ... and fast," said Bluebell. She looked from fairy face to fairy face but everyone stared blankly back at her. No one had any bright ideas.

But then Snowdrop said, "Fairy flying can't be that different from bird flying, can it?"

Bluebell looked puzzled but Daisy instantly understood what she was thinking. "Maybe we could teach him!" she cried. "Good thinking, Snowdrop!" As Snowdrop smiled shyly, Daisy turned to Rosehip. "Do you think it might work?" she asked.

Rosehip looked thoughtful. "Well, birds and fairies are very different," she said slowly, "but I suppose we both have wings. It might just work. And besides, what choice do we have?"

"That's settled then," squealed Bluebell with excitement. "We'll give him fairy flying lessons!"

As Rosehip comforted Lucky and explained to him what they were going to do, Katie drew a runway line down the grass outside the Fairy House with some white chalk from her craft kit. Bluebell and Daisy made poles from twigs and Snowdrop tied some polka dot material on to them to make flags.

They were all very excited about teaching Lucky to fly again.

When everything was ready,

Katie planted the flags at either end of the runway and they all stood at one end with Lucky. They were going to join in the lesson with him so he didn't feel like he was doing it on his own.

Rosehip got them all to flap their wings to warm up. Katie had to flap her arms instead, but she didn't mind, because joining in was so much fun. Then they did two skips and a hop, then two skips and two hops. Next they tried a hop, a skip and a flap, and then two, and then three, and then suddenly Rosehip shouted, "UP!"

On the third hop the fairies all sprang into the air. They flew a little way and Katie ran alongside them, but Lucky only just lifted off the ground. Still, it was good for a first try, so they all clapped and cheered for him.

All except Bluebell, that was.

Instead she put her hands on her hips and tossed her bright blue hair. "You know what, Rosehip," she announced, "I think you're going too slowly. Look how well he lifted into the air. I reckon if we just—"

Rosehip frowned at her. "Bluebell, I know what I'm doing," she hissed.

"But let me just try something," said Bluebell.

"Bluebell, if we want to help Lucky, it's really important that we work together," Katie insisted. "Like when we all carried the worm. Rosehip understands him best, so let's just. . ."

But impatient Bluebell ignored her. "Come on, it's easy," she said to Lucky, who looked at her in puzzlement. "Just flap your wings and go!" she cried. "Like this!"

"Bluebell. . ." Katie warned, but Bluebell flapped her wings and zoomed into the air. Then she touched down beside Lucky and cried, "Your turn now! Go, go!"

Lucky suddenly seemed to understand. He flapped his wings furiously and lifted off the ground. Bluebell threw Rosehip a triumphant glare. "See, he's doing it!" she cried. "I told you I was ri—"

But then Lucky looked down and squealed in panic. He began to flap too fast, unbalancing himself.

"Aaahhhh!!!" cried Katie and the fairies. They threw themselves to the ground and rolled out of the way as Lucky came crashing down. He went rolling along in the grass with a skitter and a squawk. Rosehip rushed over and gave him a hug, checking him over and

pulling the leaves and bits of grass off his feathers. "It's all right, little one," she sang soothingly in bird language. "It's OK."

When Bluebell approached them, Lucky tried to hide behind Rosehip, although of course he didn't fit. He whimpered and gave Bluebell a baleful look.

"I'll just go and find another worm, shall I?" mumbled Bluebell, and off she shuffled, looking very ashamed of herself.

Even after Bluebell had brought Lucky another worm, and said sorry lots of times, he was still too scared to try flying again.

Katie wondered how she could make him feel more confident. Suddenly she remembered about the conker case helmets they had worn to ride the magic ponies.

"One second, I'll be right back," she called. She dashed into the Fairy House and up to Rosehip's room, where she found the spiky green helmets under the bed. She grabbed one and hurried back outside.

She handed it to Rosehip who grinned and said "Good idea," then strapped it on to Lucky's head. Eager to have a good idea too, Snowdrop dragged her mattress out of the Fairy House and put it up at the far end of the runway. That way Lucky could land on them if he did come crashing out of the sky again. He had a little jump up and down on it and knocked his conker case helmet against one of the flagpoles

56

to test it out. Then he called out to Rosehip that he felt brave enough to have another go.

And so the second fairy flying lesson began.

Katie and the fairies and Lucky all did the skipping and hopping and flapping together, and when Rosehip called "UP!" the fairies zoomed into the air. Lucky managed to get off the ground for a second, and they all gave him a big clap and cheer, especially Bluebell.

After lots and lots of hopping and skipping and flapping practice, Rosehip nodded thoughtfully. Then she smiled and said, "Right. I think he's ready now. It's time to fly."

She whispered words of encouragement to Lucky. The fairies stood to the side, beaming at him and trying not to show

how nervous they felt.

Rosehip gave the signal and he began to skip and hop along, and then he squeezed his eyes shut and flapped his wings. He lifted off the ground and they were all just about to cheer when he looked down and screeched in alarm. He pedalled his legs in mid-air but forgot to flap his wings . . . and down he came with a crash on to the mattresses!

Trembling, he hopped over to Rosehip and she stroked his feathers. "It's OK, good try," she said gently. "Have another go, you'll get it this time."

Lucky was unsure, but with lots of encouragement he tried again. He got up into the air but then felt frightened again. He forgot to flap his wings, and down he came.

After that he refused to even try. Instead he curled himself up on the grass and began to wail and wail, a wail that Katie knew meant, "I want my mummy!"

A tear ran down Rosehip's cheek. "I just don't know what else to do," she sniffled. The others all huddled round and tried to comfort her.

They couldn't think of what to do either.

If Lucky couldn't fly, they really had no idea how to get him back

to his mum and dad.

"Oh, this is awful!" wailed Rosehip.
But just then, things got a lot worse.
A long dark shadow engulfed them.
The cat was back.

Chapter 5

The cat stared at them and slowly blinked its yellow eyes.

They all gazed back at it, hardly daring to breathe.

Through her terror, Katie thought fast. If she could just get to the door handle and turn herself big again she could easily scoop Lucky up and chase the cat away.

She began to shuffle towards the Fairy House, but even that small movement was too much. The cat

pounced. As Katie shrieked and rolled out of the way, the fairies scattered into the air in panic. Poor Lucky was left on the ground, all alone. The cat went slinking towards him, right between Katie and the Fairy House. She knew that there was no way she could make it to the door handle now. She crouched under a dock leaf, trembling, desperately trying to think of what to do next.

The fairies were swooping down as low as they dared, trying to distract the cat by pulling faces and shouting. The cat hissed at them, but then it

turned back to Lucky. In desperation, Bluebell flew down low and just above the cat's head, waving her arms and kicking her legs. They all gasped in horror as the cat took a swipe at her and knocked her out of the air. She tumbled over and over and landed in a heap by the bath tub. Suddenly Katie had an idea. Looking at the bath had reminded her that cats don't like water.

"Quick, Rosehip, distract it for me!" she cried.

Rosehip span and danced in the air above the cat, taking care not to get too close. The cat yowled and pranced about on its hind legs, trying to swipe her out of the air too. Katie made a run for it and crouched down beside the bath full of water, next to Bluebell. She whispered her plan to the little fairy,

and together they began to heave at the bath tub. It was far too heavy, but luckily the other fairies realized what they were doing and flew over to help. As the cat went for Lucky again they all pushed as hard as they could. The bath tipped up and all the water splashed out on to the cat.

"Yeek!" it screeched. It forgot about Lucky and rounded on the five friends instead.

Katie screamed.

"Don't worry, I've got you," called Rosehip. She grabbed Katie's hand and zoomed into the air. Katie was pulled off the ground, but then her wet hand slithered out of Rosehip's and she fell back to earth with a thud.

She caught her breath, and stared in horror at the cat. It was

completely focused on the terrified bird again, about to pounce.

Without even thinking, Katie leapt right in front of Lucky, shielding him as best she could. As he whimpered behind her, she stared at the cat, panic thrumming in her chest. It was so close, she could feel its breath on her face. And she could see its sharp white teeth.

The fairies were fluttering just above its head, desperately trying to distract it, but it was totally focused on Katie and Lucky. It swayed on its hind legs, ready to pounce. In that split second, terrible thoughts flashed through Katie's mind. How she was never going to see Mum again. How Mum would never find out what had happened to her. She shuddered with fright and desperately tried to come up with a plan, but she was all out of ideas.

The cat yowled and licked its lips.

A moment later she heard Rosehip above them, talking in bird language. Then the fairies all joined in, in English, calling, "You can do it. Hop hop, flap flap, remember? Come on, clever bird, brave bird, give it a try!"

They were telling Lucky to fly! He

looked at Katie and although she was very scared too she managed to give him a nod of encouragement. Lucky began to hop and flap. . .

But the movement made the cat pounce.

Katie screamed as she felt sharp claws rush past her ear. It had just missed her. But it wasn't giving up that easily.

"Hop, hop, flap, flap!" she cried, as the cat got ready to strike again.

Lucky screwed up his face in concentration and hopped and flapped.

The cat pounced again.

Its claws were crashing down right on top of them now. There was nothing more to be done. Katie hugged Lucky, squeezed her eyes shut and waited for the blow to strike. She heard the thud of the

cat's claws on the ground ... but she didn't feel anything.

She opened one eye and gasped. Lucky had lifted them into the air! She clung to his neck as he flapped his wings furiously. She squeezed her eyes shut, expecting them to drop to the ground again at any second, but instead her stomach flipped as they soared higher and

higher. She clambered on to Lucky's back and then they were zooming through the air, with the fairies alongside them, cheering.

Katie gripped his feathers tightly and looked down to see the cat leaping into the air, hissing angrily. They'd escaped! Lucky had saved her life! She laughed out loud – hardly able to believe it. She was flying! Flying high in the air on the back of a bird!

Lucky called out in delight too, and Katie guessed that he meant, "I'm flying, I'm flying!"

Rosehip sang something in bird language and the other fairies cried, "Yes, you're really flying! Well done, Lucky, well done!"

Katie was just about to ask if any of them had thought where they might be going when something

even more amazing happened. High in the air over the almost-meadow, Lucky suddenly changed direction. He also began to sing a different song.

"He knows where the nest is," Rosehip cried. "He can see more from up here, and he's spotted it! Come on!" And with that the fairies turned in mid-air and followed him all the way home.

Chapter 6

After a thrilling, stomach-flipping flight, Katie and Lucky and the fairies touched down in the empty nest, high in the tree tops.

Katie clambered off Lucky's back and took off his helmet. Then she had a big hug with her fairy friends. They hugged Lucky too. Then they all stroked Lucky and told him how clever he was. He shook his feathers in delight and looked very, *very* proud of himself.

They all gazed round the nest in amazement.

It was beautiful, glittering with an array of treasures, from tinfoil tart cases to toffee wrappers.

"Oh, I remember now," Katie gasped. "Magpies like to pick up anything shiny and use it to make their nests." Just then, something extra special caught her eye that

looked like ... maybe ... But she didn't have time to get closer and find out what it was, because Lucky began to wail loudly.

They all knew he was calling for his mummy. They glanced at each other. "We should probably go before his parents arrive," said Snowdrop, looking nervous, and even Rosehip agreed.

"But how am I going to fly back without Lucky?" cried Katie in panic. "None of you are strong enough to carry me!"

The fairies looked panicked. They hadn't thought of that. Two large sleek black and white magpies were gliding towards them. Katie shuddered. "Quick! Fly away!" she hissed to her friends.

But no one moved.

Bluebell folded her arms and

said, "We're not going without you. We're all sticking together."

"Go, now, please. . ." Katie begged, but still no one moved, although they were all looking very frightened.

The father magpie circled nearby, calling loudly. They all squealed and ducked as the mother magpie came flapping right over their heads and landed on the side of the nest, gripping on with her curved talons. Then she gave a cry and did a squawky flappy huggy dance with Lucky.

"Aw!" said Daisy, "they're back together! That's so sweet!"

But then the mother magpie turned to them. Katie and the fairies huddled together as she regarded them with her hard black eyes. Her beak was very, very sharp indeed. Katie hugged Daisy tight. "I hope

Lucky can explain what we're doing in her nest!" she whispered, "and quickly!"

They all held their breath as Lucky went *chacker-chacker-chacker*, saying something to his mother. Then they sighed with relief as the look in her eyes softened. Katie and the fairies gave her nervous smiles. She called out and Rosehip translated.

"It's OK. She's thanking us for saving her baby," she told them. They all smiled nervously and Bluebell said, "Oh, it was no trouble, apart from when I almost got eaten by that cat!" That made them all laugh and at last they relaxed.

Then the mother magpie was saying something else to Rosehip. "She's inviting us to choose one of

her treasures as a thank you," she told her friends.

Katie was about to say, "there's no need" without thinking, but then she looked more closely at the glittering nest. She remembered the something that she had spotted before, that she'd thought, maybe. . .

Yes, there it was: a silver bracelet was twined among the twigs and grasses and sweet wrappers and tinfoil. She looked to the mother magpie, who shook her feathers and nodded her head slightly. Katie gently pulled the bracelet out of the woven grass and brushed away the mud. She felt her stomach flip with excitement. "Yes, it is!" she gasped.

"Yes it is what?" asked Bluebell impatiently.

Katie grinned. "Can't you tell?"

The fairies all gathered round and

peered at the bracelet. It was set with a bright green gem. "That's an emerald!" cried Snowdrop suddenly. "One of the birthstones we need to finish the fairy task and save the Magic Oak tree. Wow!"

Katie held up the bracelet and the mother magpie nodded her head. They all squealed in delight and thanked her again and again.

"There's still the problem of how to get me home," said Katie, suddenly feeling very glum again. Saving Lucky from the cat and finding another birthstone and escaping to the nest weren't much use if she could never get back to

the almost-meadow.

But Snowdrop had had another one of her brilliant ideas. She told Katie to sit on the bracelet as if it were a swing and to hold on tight with both hands. Then she got Rosehip and Bluebell to hover in the air and hold the bracelet tightly. "Can you lift that?" she asked them.

They had a go and could just about manage the weight.

They all hugged Lucky goodbye and it took a long time for Rosehip to let go of her feathered friend.

Then, "One, two, three – lift off!" cried Rosehip and Bluebell together. They leaped off the side of the nest and Katie squealed in delight as she was lifted into the air on her special swing. Then she called goodbye to Lucky and his mother, and Daisy and Snowdrop waved. Katie held

tight to the bracelet as she swung around in the air. It was such an exciting ride – just as exciting as being on Lucky's back!

By the time they touched down at the Fairy House, Katie was red-cheeked and giggling. She and the fairies took hold of the necklace and danced round and round with it,

spinning and twirling.

"I can't believe we found another birthstone!" sang Rosehip.

"We only need four more and we can work the magic to save the tree and all of Fairyland with it!" added Daisy.

Then they all sang "Well done, Rosehip!" over and over again until the little flame-haired fairy was blushing and giggling so much she collapsed on the ground in a heap. They all leapt on her and had a big, silly, giggly fairy hug together.

When they had finally stopped giggling and picked themselves up, they carried the emerald bracelet upstairs and hid it in Snowdrop's wardrobe for safe-keeping.

"That's much easier than carrying a wriggly worm," Bluebell declared, making them all laugh.

"When I go home I'll take it back with me and put it safely in my jewellery box with the other birthstones we've collected," Katie promised them.

Bluebell looked thoughtful, "We'll have to watch out for that cat in future," she said. "I think I'll make a lookout post on the roof. I could sprinkle some spiders' webs with fairy dust and weave them around the meadow so that a magical alarm goes off if that cat touches them. What do you think, Rosehip?"

Rosehip grinned at her. "That sounds like a brilliant idea, Bluebell," she said. "Shall we start now? What would you like us to do?"

Bluebell grinned, delighted to be in charge again. "Well, if Daisy and I go looking for spiders' webs, you and Katie could gather some twigs to make the lookout post, and Snowdrop could find us something to make a bell. . ."

As Bluebell chatted away, Rosehip winked at Katie and Katie couldn't help smiling!

Then they all joined hands and went skipping and tumbling back outside into the sunshine.

The End

Bluebell
Spring fairy

Likes:

blue, blue, blue and more blue,
turning somersaults in the air, dancing

Dislikes:

coming second, being told what to do

Daisy
Summer fairy

Likes:

everyone to be friends, bright sunshine,
cheery yellow colours, smiling

Dislikes:

arguments, cold dark places,
orange nylon dresses

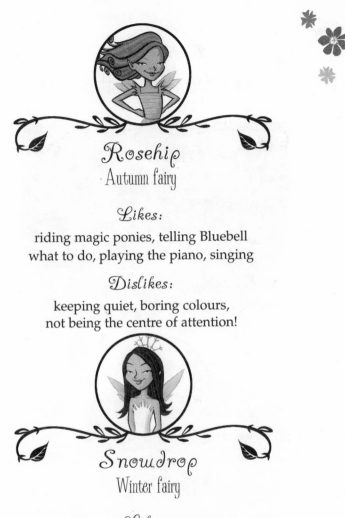

Rosehip
Autumn fairy

Likes:

riding magic ponies, telling Bluebell
what to do, playing the piano, singing

Dislikes:

keeping quiet, boring colours,
not being the centre of attention!

Snowdrop
Winter fairy

Likes:

singing fairy songs, cool quiet places, riding her
favourite magical unicorn, making snowfairies

Dislikes:

being too hot, keeping secrets

Look out for more Fairy House books!

The Fairy House

Fairy Friends

Kelly McKain

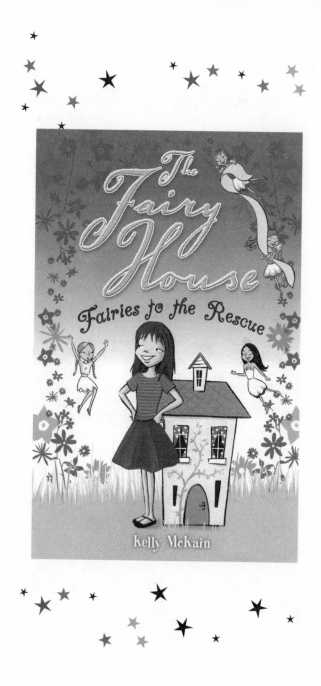

The Fairy House

Fairies to the Rescue

Kelly McKain